D1030045

Ongwe oweh oadeh sigwa .... deh
weso sigwa neh ga-ya-dos-hah dio ·
FULTON PUBLIC LIBRARY
FULTON · NEW YORK

Heather Hiding

by Nancy White Carlstrom   illustrated by Dennis Nolan

Macmillan Publishing Company   New York
Collier Macmillan Publishers   London

Macmillan Publishing Company
866 Third Avenue, New York, NY 10022
Collier Macmillan Canada, Inc.
Printed and bound in Singapore
First American Edition

10 9 8 7 6 5 4 3 2 1

The text of this book is set in 14 point Sabon.
The illustrations are rendered in watercolor on paper.

Library of Congress Cataloging-in-Publication Data
Carlstrom, Nancy White.
Heather hiding/by Nancy White Carlstrom;
illustrated by Dennis Nolan.
– 1st American Ed. p. cm.
Summary: Wishing she were taller and faster,
like her big brother Peter, Heather plays
hide-and-seek with him and his friends and
demonstrates how good she is at hiding.
ISBN 0-02-717370-4
[1. Hide-and-seek – Fiction. 2. Brothers and sisters – Fiction.]
I. Nolan, Dennis, ill. II. Title.
PZ7.C21684He 1989 [E] – dc19 88-8286 CIP AC

For Barbara Goldin
and our Seattle Writing Group
Margaret, Cathy, Pat, Chris,
Nancy, Eileen, and Linda
with love and thanks
– N.W.C.

For all the Nolan girls
– D.N.

Heather is small. She wants to be taller.
Heather is slow. She wants to run faster.

“Like Peter,” she says.

Big brother Peter can do everything well.

He climbs higher, jumps farther, runs faster than anyone.

What can Heather do?
She sits watching. She sits waiting.

Peter says, “Let’s play hide-and-seek. I’ll close my eyes. I won’t peek. Hurry now, I’m counting.”

All the others run.

Heather stands up. Where can she hide?

Behind a tree, like a bushy-tailed squirrel?
Inside a tree, like a sleepy-faced owl?
Up in a tree, like a fluffy-winged bird?

Heather has to hide well and not tell anyone.

Heather hunts and Heather finds
a tiny space just right for her. The very best hiding place.

Will Peter see her? He won't hear.
Heather's still as a baby deer
in a meadow crossing.
Quiet as grass growing,
silent as a spider spinning.

Heather sitting hears birdsong in the trees.
Heather waiting counts all the things she sees.

Three ladybugs, two bees, four dandelions, six ferns.
Heather hiding slowly turns.
Five daisies, one stone.

Heather's drowsy, getting warm.
One sun, three clouds, two sheep.
Heather hiding falls asleep.

Tall Peter, fast Peter,
at last Peter finds everyone.

Meagan and Jason, Rachel and Chris.
Someone is missing. It's Heather.

"Allee, allee in free!
Come out, come out, wherever you are.
Come, Heather. You've won, Heather."

She's so small and so slow.
She can't be far.
Where could Heather go?

Find Heather hiding.

The sun is sliding from its high sky chair.

Cool shadows nudge Heather awake.
She doesn't budge until she hears big brother Peter.

He's calling, calling,
in a not-so-tall,
it-matters-after-all voice.

“Come, Heather.
I won’t run fast, Heather.”

Peter's closer. Now he passes.
Heather listening in the grasses hears him whisper,
"Please come, Heather."

"I'm here. I'm here."
Heather shouts and gets up slowly.

Heather hiding is Heather found.

Peter looks down, proud of her,
and says real loud,
"Heather is good at hiding!"